Maylis de Kerangal

Eastbound

TRANSLATED FROM THE FRENCH BY
Jessica Moore

archipelago books

Copyright © Maylis de Kerangal
Originally published as *Tangente vers l'est* by Editions Gallimard, Paris, 2012
English language translation © Jessica Moore, 2023

First Archipelago Books Edition, 2023

Library of Congress Cataloging-in-Publication Data available upon request.
ISBN 9781953861504 (paperback) | ISBN 9781953861511 (ebook)

Archipelago Books
232 3rd Street #A111
Brooklyn, NY 11215
www.archipelagobooks.org

Distributed by Penguin Random House
www.penguinrandomhouse.com

Cover photo: *Rushing Train* by Hakuyō Fuchikami
Cover design by Zoe Guttenplan
Book design by Gopa & Ted2, Inc.

This work is made possible by the New York State Council on the Arts with the
support of the Office of the Governor and the New York State Legislature.

This publication received financial support from the Cultural Services of the
French Embassy in the United States through their publishing assistance programs.

Funding for the publication of this book was provided by a grant
from the Carl Lesnor Family Foundation.

Archipelago Books also gratefully acknowledges the generous support of
Lannan Foundation, the National Endowment for the Arts, the Nimick
Forbesway Foundation, the New York City Department of Cultural Affairs,
Jan Michalski Foundation, and Centre National du Livre.
This work received support for excellence in publication and translation
from Albertine Translation, a program created by Villa Albertine
and funded by FACE Foundation.

Printed in the United States
Fourth Printing

EASTBOUND

THESE GUYS come from Moscow and don't know where they're going. There's a crowd of them, more than a hundred, young, white—pallid, even—wan and shorn, their arms veiny and eyes pacing the train car, camouflage pants and briefs, torsos caged in khaki undershirts, thin chains with crosses bouncing against their chests; guys lining the walls in the passageways and corridors, sitting, standing, stretched out on the berths, letting their arms dangle, their feet dangle, letting their bored resignation dangle in the void. They've been on board for more than forty hours now, crammed together, squeezed into the liminal space of the train: the conscripts.

3

As the train nears the station, they get up and crush against the windows, press their faces to the panes or rush to squeeze up against the doors, and then jostle for more room, crane to see something outside, limbs tangled and necks outstretched as though there wasn't enough air, a mass of squid—but it's strange, if they get out to smoke on the platform or stretch their legs they never stray very far, stay clumped together in front of the steps—a herd—and shrug when people ask where they're headed: they've been told Krasnoyarsk and Barnaoul, they've been told Chita, but it always comes down to the same thing: no one tells them anything. General Smirnov may well have said that things were changing, in televised press conferences, that from now on, out of respect for the families, conscripts would know where they were to be posted, but still it seems that once you get beyond Novosibirsk, Siberia remains that which it always has been: a limit-experience. A gray zone. Here or there, then, what difference does it make? Here or there, it's all the same. And then the kits are handed out and everyone is hustled on board the Trans-Siberian and off they go.

Next come the irreversible rails, laying out the countryside, unfolding, unfolding, unfolding Russia, pressing on between latitudes 50° N and 60° N, and the guys who grow sticky in the wagons, scalps pale beneath the tonsure, temples glistening with sweat, and among them Aliocha, twenty years old, his build strong but his body caught in contrary impulses—torso skewed forward while the shoulders are thrust back, choleric, complexion like mortar, black eyes. He's posted at the far end of the train, at the back of the last wagon in a compartment slathered in thick paint, a cell, pierced by three openings, that the smokers have seized immediately. This is where he's found himself a spot, a volume of space still unoccupied, notched between other bodies. He has pressed his forehead to the back window of the train, the one that looks out over the tracks, and stays there watching the land speed by at 60km/h—in this moment it's a wooly mauve wilderness, his shitty country.

Right up until the last, Aliocha had believed he wouldn't have to go. Right up until April 1st, the traditional day of the Spring Draft, he thought he would manage to avoid military service, to fake out the system and be exempted—and to tell the truth, there's not a single guy in Moscow between eighteen and twenty-seven years old who hasn't tried to do the same. It's the young men of means who tend to be favored at this game; the others do what they can, and meanwhile their mothers scream in Pushkin Square, in ever-increasing numbers since the soldier Sytchev was martyred, and gather around Valentina Melnikova, President of the Committee of Soldiers' Mothers—they're fearsome, boiling mad, determined, and if the cameras turn up they rush to fit their eager faces in the frame: I don't want my son to go, and he's not even a drinker! When reprieves run out, the next option is the false medical certificate, bought for an arm and a leg from doctors who slip the cash directly into their breast pockets, and the families who've been bled dry go home and get smashed in relief. If this doesn't work, and when anxiety has bitten down night after night to the quick, then come the direct attempts at bribery. These can be effective but slow to put into action and meanwhile time is galloping past—investigating the networks of influence within administrations, identifying the right person, the one who'll be able to intervene, all this takes a crazy amount of time. And finally, when there's nothing left, when it's looking hopeless, there are women. Find one before winter and get her knocked up—this is all that's left to do because at six months a pregnancy will grant an exemption. So there's no time to lose, the guys get worked up, the women too, not wanting to see their sweetheart leave for military service—might as well say go to war—or coveting conjugal salvation when most of them are single and ashamed

7

of it. Things heat up and soon the condoms are tossed aside, the act is done on squeaking mattresses, and they stick it to the army—they give it the finger.

A girlfriend to save me, that's where Aliocha was at six months ago—Aliocha who doesn't have a mother anymore and no money. So night after night he shaved, slicked back his hair with drugstore gel and put on his best threads—snail-like operations, hesitant gestures, little conviction—and went out into the hard night, slowing as he passed the bars to slant a glance inside, into their black and red depths, lingering in the fast-food joints, and ending up in a club with a neighbor younger than him, a twisted little thug who gets in for free everywhere and who urges him to act, voice shrill in Aliocha's ear, go on, you've gotta make an effort, she's not just gonna fall in your lap, his expert eye scanning the bodies entwined in the spasms of techno, bodies to which Aliocha had his back turned, standing at the bar with his neck sunk between his shoulders, back hunched, nose in the bottom of a glass of whisky he can't afford. Soon all he did was wander through the giant city where he lived with his grandmother, sitting in staircases, waiting in the courtyards of apartment buildings: he had given up, abandoned the thing that had never begun, this humiliation, this scheme. No woman had ever come to save him, not even the one who walked through the schoolyard in his dreams, fatal and serene, long red wool coat, black leather gloves, gray fur chapka, blonde hair beneath: a planet unto herself. No, especially not her.

They left Novossibirsk and the enormous central station, high walls of a milky green, tiled hall with the acoustics of a city pool—an icy temple. Aliocha is scared. Siberia—fuck! This is what he's thinking, stone in his belly, as though seized with panic at the idea of plunging further into what he knows to be a territory of banishment, giant oubliette of the Tsarist empire before it turns Gulag country. A forbidden perimeter, a silent space, faceless. A black hole. The cadence of the train, monotonous, rather than numbing his anxiety, shakes it up and revives it, unspools lines of deportees pickaxes in hand stumbling through swirling snowstorms, stirs the frail shacks lined up in the middle of nowhere, hair frozen to wooden floor planks in the night, dead bodies stiff under the permafrost, blurred images of a territory from which no one returns. Outside, the afternoon is drawing to a close, in a few hours it will be night, but this night won't be populated with human dreams, Aliocha knows this too. Nothing here is on the human scale, nothing familiar will welcome him here—and it's this, even, that terrorizes him, this continental pocket in the interior of the continent, this enclave bordered only by the immensity. A finite but edgeless space—consistent, oddly enough, with the representation astrophysicists give of the universe itself—all of this scares the hell out of him. It's not hard to understand, it *is* terrifying, and Aliocha's heart wallops in his chest as the train chugs along at a constant speed just like the boy's terror will, from here on in: at the end of the rails, there will be the barracks and the *diedovchina*, the hazing, and once he's there, if the second-year conscripts burn his dick with cigarettes, if they make him lick the toilets, deprive him of sleep or fuck him up the ass, no one will be able to do anything to help.

Some guys have just come in and are already forming a circle, joking about bitches and benders, their faces red, eyes glassy, and when the train shudders they laugh, thrown off balance, grab hold of whatever they can, usually each other, clinging together, crashing into each other. Aliocha smokes like a maniac—*papirossys*, rustic cigarettes with a cardboard cylinder for a filter—tossing them sidelong glances, thinking it's time he took his place among them feet planted wide beer in hand, time he told his own little story too. But he wouldn't know how, wouldn't know what to say because he's twenty and still a virgin—even if he did sleep with the planet-girl, holding her in his arms, stretched out on his back with her head tucked into the curve of his shoulder, lips parted at exactly the level of his armpit and her breath like a flow of heat radiating across his whole body, her hair spread out—a virgin, then, and rather sober. Wait, let yourself be forgotten, melt like a chameleon among the others, become transparent— Aliocha crouches down, head tucked between his shoulders, retracts his neck, glues his eyes to his knees, I'm not here, I don't exist—in this moment he's like little kids playing hide-and-seek who cover their eyes instead of hiding, convinced they are invisible if they themselves can't see anything.

When he finally lifts his head, Aliocha's eyes blink rapidly beneath the bare bulb of the compartment. The light lacquers the partitions painted military gray where shadows shape themselves, the room is as close as a dungeon and all the more cramped, all the more overcrowded as the space around it expands, emptying out as the train plunges ahead, charging into the plain. Run away. The idea suddenly goes through the boy, a flash of lightning-like certainty tangible as a stone, and at this exact moment the Trans-Siberian rushes into a tunnel, run away, get out as fast as possible, defect, jump.

It's the end of the afternoon and the sky is turning to ash. The back window is free again and Aliocha leaps to it, magnetized to this unique focal point on the world— like an eye in the back of your head—captivated by the sight of the tracks that hurtle backwards into the landscape, striped ribbon alternating light and dark, stroboscope lighting up his face, and soon, hypnotized, he touches the point in space where the forest swallows the still-hot rails, engulfs the ties in a well of mystery, bit by bit he forgets the train car, forgets the guys smoking behind him and the smell of skin suctioned to the walls from sweat, all he is now is this vanishing point that devours space and time; he coincides with it, grows obsessed, ready to pour himself too into the great black hole, to tumble in headfirst, anything but Siberia, anything but the barracks, so concentrated in this moment that he doesn't hear the two guys coming up behind him, bellies out jostling him, sandwiching him, then pushing roughly and pressing him against the wall as though trying to shove his body into it. Aliocha groans, twisted, his profile burns against the wall of glass, a wound, his Adam's apple is going to split and crumble, danger grows sharper, these two are gonna kill him, take him down and sit on his chest, spit in his face, drool on his eyelids, one of them is already sticking his tongue into his ear while the other whispers through thick breath, you done hogging the window yet? Go on, get outta here. They finally let go and take a step back while Aliocha stands up, catches his breath, but he's not off the hook, no escape yet: the two conscripts take turns hitting him, one punch each on the nape of his neck that hurl him forward, his nose bashing into the window once, twice, blood spurting out. And then it stops. Aliocha waits, eyes half-closed, then slowly turns around: the two guys are still there, doubled over laughing. He's alone with them, the others have all gone to sprawl onto bunks way too narrow for their growing bodies. He tries to get past them and they push him back limply, still cracking up, bodies loose with paroxysms, he's trying to get away from them when he catches sight of himself in the glass—the window's become a mirror, darkened by a complicit tunnel: he is tall and knows he's strong, a strength you wouldn't suspect in a body like his. Slowly he loads the fist, pulling back the elbow to gain good momentum and then *bam*, he punches one of them in the face, an uppercut to the temple of such force that the guy staggers and falls, freeing up a pathway. Aliocha steps through and heads swiftly back to his car, while the other conscript, arms dangling, looks at his friend lying there among puddles of beer and cigarette butts, looks him up and down, expressionless, and then even he gives him a kick in the side, turns on his heel and abandons him there.

Aliocha locks himself in the first bathroom that's free, washes the blood from his face with plenty of water, examines the marks, makes himself a compress by tearing a length of toilet paper from the huge roll attached to the wall and soaks it in ice-cold water before pressing it to his red profile, his swollen nose. And then, ignoring the insults shouted by people waiting outside, their kicks against the door, he takes his time checking the mirror to make sure his face is slowly regaining its color and volume. But his bruises mark him out now as a victim, he knows it, and once he's out of the bathroom he seeks out the shadows, the darkness, and reaches his train car by slinking along the walls.

Back in his bunk, he mulls things over. The train is long, about fifteen cars: two first class, three or four second, the *koupeinë* (compartment cars), the restaurant, and then all the rest, third class, the *platskartnye* (non-compartmented cars), modest families and the members of the troop congealed in the miasma of a permanent picnic; there you'll find those crossing the entire country or in transit from one godforsaken town to another—inheritance, a move, a visit to a sick relative, a birth, a marriage, a burial in one of those tiny cemeteries on the outskirts surrounded by a thin blue metal fence, a medical appointment—drunk men who do nothing but doze, children so wound up they can't fall asleep—they just bounce off the walls, infants bawling in their mothers' arms (a hot, exhausted woman who won't sleep a wink, her feet swollen in plastic sandals bought specially for the trip). People play cards while cutting up cold chicken and smoked fish, they drink vodka because there's nothing else to do, they fill in crosswords mechanically, they tappety-tap on cell phones, and, finally, they don't even look outside, not even a glance. Aliocha could easily hide in here, in these overcrowded cars: who would notice his absence? The soldiers would get out at their destination and he would continue on, hidden. Or maybe he'd take advantage of a stop in some station to hightail it outta there: the guys would get out on the platform, he'd follow the crowd, pretend to be buying a pack of smokes, step away quickly and erase himself into the darkness while dodging the slow rounds of the night watchmen.

He straightens up, torso vertical—an electric kick; he wants to know now where and when the train will stop. Slides off the bunk in search of the placards that list the stops en route. Paces the third class, inspects the signs, finds nothing, retraces his steps, runs into the *provodnitsa*, the hostess in charge of the car, cinched military-style in a straight skirt while the peroxide blond of her hair overplays the Russian beauty, she's still up at this hour of night, a broom in hand, bucket in the other—someone must have puked somewhere—and gathering up his momentum he asks her directly: excuse me, when is the next stop? His voice is false, the sly looseness of the cat plotting a move. The woman stops short, lifts her head and casts him a glance, slowly puts the broom down, the bucket, dries her hands flat on her blouse, down over her thighs, then shoots back: what do you want? She's spoken too loudly, Aliocha shivers, heads will end up turning toward them, heads that are never fully asleep, and among them the head of fat-assed Sergeant Letchov who prowls constantly, sly as a threat. Aliocha lowers his head and asks again, quieter: when is the next stop? The woman comes closer—her face is lit in the neon light of the hallway, oily, puffy, her blond hair aquarium-shaded, greenish, her small eyes lined with turquoise, she comes up so close that he can smell her skin—cloying scent of ginger and face powder—and then, standing on tiptoe, she casts a glance over the boy's shoulder to make sure no one's coming down the hall. She knows perfectly well what he has in mind, this one, she's known it since she first started working on the Trans-Siberian, since forever.

Aliocha wobbles: the *provodnitsa* gets it, and now he's at her mercy, there's nothing to stop her from going to see Letchov and saying, hey, there's a guy acting all weird over there, a guy asking a lot of questions. Instead of which her eyes hold firm to the boy's and she says in a breath the next stop is Krasnoyarsk at 10 pm, we're stopping for twenty minutes, the station is huge, there will be patrols. Aliocha nods, thanks, but the woman is already turning her back and busying herself with the samovar, full hips and round belly contained inside the barrel of her skirt, breasts compressed beneath the white shirt that is—uncannily—still impeccable at this hour. He goes back to his bunk.

So an hour to wait, barely an hour, at the end of which he'll attempt an escape. Aliocha lies stretched out now, strangely calm. No longer is the future like an inert and viscous landscape, a long corridor of dirty snow: he has a plan and this is enough to make him relax, to slow his pulse and ease his anxiety. The train car is no longer this stifling chamber, a space of confinement with stale air, but is now a car pierced by four doors—two at each end—and similarly, the conscripts are no longer potential enemies but allies: when it's time to get out on the platform, he will be one with them, will match their movements and laugh at their jokes, he'll melt into the mass.

The sound of steps through the car, the thwack of plastic sandals, Aliocha jumps: the *provodnitsa* has come in. He makes her out as she heads towards the bunk where Letchov is sleeping, her blondness washing out a halo in the dark above the nightlight clipped to her shirt. Whispering, she tries to rouse the sergeant who finally sways towards her, groaning. He sits up, rubs his eyes, questions her with a jut of his chin and she steps back as though scared, and now they're talking together in low voices, she leaning over with hands tucked between her knees and forehead near the sergeant's as he nods his head and murmurs. Aliocha doesn't hear them, but he convinces himself that she's describing him, and now Letchov squints in his direction as the boy instinctively closes his eyes, feigning innocent sleep. He closes his lids and lets out a long breath: the bitch! Women who live in the Trans-Siberian are two-faced, everyone knows it, what was he thinking, trusting her? He thinks back to the tiny kitchen in the communal apartment where his mother and others would linger at the table in the evenings, remembers that in their conversations these train attendants were held in high regard, people feared them as much as they envied the legendary aura that marked them out from all other Russians: cross-border agents without a passport moving from one republic to the next, these women had smuggled packages during the Soviet period, carried secrets, whispered promises, trafficked all there is to traffic, using the extraordinary privilege of being able to move around while everyone else remained still, under house arrest, and still today, their bodies split the whole of Russia across the width, from Moscow to Vladivostok and from Vladivostok to Moscow—nearly a quarter of the circumference of the earth with each trip, did you know; their skin habituated to the climate, their feet have felt the earth's relief, the least rise in the contour line stretching over more than nine thousand kilometers, their eyes have seen wild irises and forbidden villages—clouded in coal with names that don't even appear on maps—they know the taiga, dark and golden like an infinite underbrush, they know the steppe, they know the great rivers, the Volga, the Yenisey and the Amur, and Aliocha gauges all this while staring at the woman who's disappearing now down the long shadowed corridor as Letchov falls heavily back onto his bunk; he follows with his eyes this woman who intimidates him, whose gravid body contains the entire country.

Aliocha looks at his watch. In just twenty minutes it'll be the Krasnoyarsk station, the thick night, opaque without being black—and whether this night is a friend or an enemy, again he can't be sure. Right now each of his movements works like a valve distributing two lines, symmetrical and irreconcilable, that divide in their turn, divide, divide again, plunge into a material time, a ramified future in the troubled darkness of the car, a future that harbors his freedom, Aliocha knows this, he knows nothing but this, this is his only certitude. Concentrating, he goes over the plan for his escape, reviews hypotheses and probabilities: a little before Krasnoyarsk he'll get out of his bunk and Letchov will / won't wake up; Letchov won't wake up and Aliocha will mix in with the conscripts who get out on the platform; unsteady on his legs, he'll bum a cigarette from the first guy he sees, the guy will give it to him / will refuse; the guy will refuse saying he's broke and Aliocha will reply, logically: ok, hang on, I'll go see if I can find some in the station.

And this is exactly what happens. The Trans-Siberian stops, it's Krasnoyarsk in the night, and it's an event. Disheveled, wobbly after eleven hours in the train, a few guys press together as though they were trying to fit inside each other—the good old sexual joke—about ten of them, they're not tired. On the platform they stand in circles of light drawn by the station lamps on the concrete and start smoking, stomping their big shoes on the ground, thump thump, soon they're jumping in place, tightening their collars around their warm throats, re-buttoning their sleeves at the wrist, sur-prised by the cold of these April nights when Siberia still drags its feet in winter, swollen, river frozen into a hard crust, mute nature, and in a flash those who feed them appear and place baskets filled with victuals at the bottom of the train steps—ham, cookies, vodka, sometimes a soup—push through the groups headfirst, jostling elbows and shoulders, or opt to surround them instead, immediately begin moving the merchandise all the while smoothing small bills between dirty fingers, bundling them quickly. They're the fauna of the platforms—women, mostly, bundled up in heavy coats (but the skin of their knees looks bare above their boots), scarves knotted under their chins and voices firm, older men with rheumy eyes, scrawny teens bent beneath the bags—the ones who paid the price in gold for the right to be there, trafficking smokes, dealing cold beer and candy—those who know the notice boards by heart— numbers, schedules, destinations. The insomniacs are already pacing the platforms, the restless calm their agitation with long strides, the players relax, the children run, here and there you'll see a young woman nursing her baby in the dimness or a guy crossing the rails to go piss somewhere far from the light, a multitude of feverish fingers tap on keyboards, and cell phone screens make faces glow white. Aliocha is there in the right place crossing his arms over his t-shirt and laughing along with the rest, a forced laugh, rough in his tight throat. He didn't put anything on before getting out, didn't take his bag for fear of attracting attention, he's the lightest he could be, nothing in his hands, nothing in his pockets, stripped of everything that would give him a name—he folded the photograph of his mother into the bottom of his shoe—but he has a cell phone, a charger and a hundred rubles; the desperate young conscript is gone, this is a different man. Because already a conscript is showing Aliocha his empty cigarette pack and lifting a thumb over his shoulder, pointing to the buildings of the station, go check there, you've got time—a glance at his watch. Aliocha nods, his plan is working like gangbusters, he turns with his hands in his pockets, above all don't make eye contact with the others, step away a few meters, these first meters are a river of ice, a desert of stones or a poisonous jungle, every trap-infested fractious zone. He walks straight ahead and is soon out of the circles of the station lights, a would-be deserter tossed out under the domed sky, sounds fading in his ear

27

as though he'd dived into the sea, the shouts get quieter and fear seizes his throat: he's in Krasnoyarsk, a city he knows nothing about and where he will have to survive, alone, forsaken, poor, without shelter—what madness is he embarking on? Doesn't he know that in hostile territory the solution is always collective? Who does he think he is? Before he runs, he still has to get past his filthy ignorance and know where he's putting his feet.

Aliocha hurries, heads for the front of the train, car after car, with the feeling of swimming against the current, slaloms between travelers spread out over the platform and latches on to the footsteps of a woman ahead of him. She's a foreigner, Aliocha can tell right away: backpack over her shoulder, honey-colored sheepskin coat, faded jeans tucked into leather boots, purple scarf that forms a textile-soft brace around her neck, and she's tall, brown curly hair cut short. She stops in front of each door and seems to squint to see the number on the cars—is she near-sighted?—she, too, heading for the front of the train, making her way calmly towards the first-class cars. Aliocha positions himself in her slip-stream, seven, eight cars they've passed now, about a hundred meters of platform, the station tower grows clearer, its lights throb, blinking out a Morse code he makes out instinctively—come, come—just as the arteries in his neck throb. And suddenly the *provodnitsa* is there, walking towards him, heavy, her face placid but with panicked eyes sending out signals like a lighthouse beam. Aliocha slows, deciphers this face three meters in front of him, eyes that stare at him wide as saucers, eyebrows lifted all the way to the hairline, forehead on alert: he's in danger, something behind him is a threat. Aliocha hesitates before turning and his heart hardens in an instant, a pebble: Letchov. Ten meters away. He's walking slowly, the steps of someone who's watching nothing and nobody, who's granting himself his little nocturnal promenade. Goddamn it what is he doing outside in the middle of the night? Aliocha salivates,

out of breath, hands on his hips, landslide in his chest—
the raging landslide of disappointment, fragmentation
and collapse. It's not even five degrees outside at this
hour, but over there the skinny streetlights are enough
to warm the space, to give it this orangey transparency,
this glow of a ball, and then the night begins to dance,
it spins once in a circle, because Letchov passes by with
his heavy steps without even seeing him, he can be heard
quietly spewing words into his phone while the *provodnitsa* pulls up short in front of Aliocha and, a rather
good actress, says loudly: there are no cigarette vendors
at the front of the train my boy, you won't find any here!
Aliocha, dumbstruck, casts a glance past her: a trio of
soldiers patrols slowly, black boots and felt pots on their
heads, the buttons of their gabardine coats catching the
light in brief flashes. He's surrounded. He turns and
heads back towards the conscripts' cars with his head
down, wanting to cry. Behind him, a few meters away,
the *provodnitsa*, straight as the letter "i"; and further,

the half-dozen curiously nonchalant military boot soles; Letchov, for his part, reaches the end of a long arcing half-circle that will land him at the entrance to the car in the precise instant when he finishes saying into his phone something to the effect of if you see him again I'll break your nose, I'll gouge out your eyes, I'll fuck you up, you know it, you know I'll do it, the words spat out, machine-gun fire into a feather pillow, and finally, he's the last one to climb back into the train car.

The train again. Monotonous rolling, cyclical clicking, axles warming up, shrieks of metal and, if you listened close, you'd also hear—like a tiny soundtrack woven into this hellhole—the torment of Aliocha's heart, there, back again in the compartment of the Trans-Siberian, back in his spot next to the window, and once again hypnotized by the rails, the short portion of tracks that are illuminated for a fraction of a second by the train's rear lights, the whitish trail that closes space again immediately in its passage, relegating it to a zone behind, unformed and pulsating, delivering it to the amniotic dark of origins.

Aliocha fears that the day is almost here. The last conscripts have all gone to sleep and he gathers himself into his solitude, bitterness stings his throat, bitterness or bad tobacco he doesn't know anymore, feels trapped in a backwash of terror and cold rage, a dirty mix: in Krasnoyarsk, escape refused him its clear line, it gave out beneath his feet. Now, he needs to hold on, buy some time, wait for the next big city where he might hide, remake himself and earn enough to get back to the west. Learn patience. Stay calm, don't do anything stupid, don't talk to anyone or get out just anyplace, for example one of those large villages the Trans-Siberian causes to spring up from the earth, the ones threaded along the tracks like beads on a necklace—wooden houses with chimneys smoking, passing silhouettes that tend the gardens, dogs that bark behind the fences—

he must renounce these isolated stations, these easy-to-search villages where he would so easily be caught. Patience, Aliocha, patience! He leans close to the glass, his gaze goes out past the reflection of his own face: the outside is compact and shadowy, oceanic. The Siberian forest is there—to sink into it would be like entering black water with stones in the bottom of his pockets, and Aliocha wants to live.

T HE DOORS slide open behind him. Someone has come into the compartment. Aliocha turns: the woman who got on in Krasnoyarsk, the foreigner, it's her. In one hand she holds a glass encased in silver mesh, and in the other, a lit cigarette. She stands in profile at a side window; she, too, is rummaging around in the night, the night that never closes completely here, but stays ambiguous, charged with an electric luminosity that always makes you think day is about to break. Aliocha observes her surreptitiously, swiveling his eyes in their sockets without moving his body: she's smoking, very calm, her face faintly shining. He's never seen women like her, awake at this time of

35

night and alone on trains transporting troops, women in men's shirts and big boots, not in Moscow; there, the ones who interest him wear skin-tight jeans and stand perched on mind-boggling heels, and they are blond, very blond, like Marilyn, a radical platinum that sets them apart from the throng of other women and they stride through the streets like movie heroines. But this one is from a whole other film. He takes note of the blue-tinged calm that infuses the compartment with the swirling volutes of her cigarette—a strange sensation. He knows when she pushes back a lock of hair, when she trails her glass against her lip—the metal refracts the light from the large bulb on the ceiling, and then there's a liquid flash—and he knows when she looks at her watch or the screen of her phone. Finally, he turns frankly to see what she looks like. They exchange a glance and the woman smiles. It's not a playful smile, nor even a complicit one, it's something else—let's call it a gesture—and Aliocha instinctively receives it as it was given. He leans back against the window. Once more the translucent opening, the rails that appear in a brief metallic flash that's swallowed up again just as quickly by the night, chalky stones crushed between cross ties, sometimes a tuft of white, powdery grass, and once more these tracks remind him: he only exists now to get away.

Abruptly, he moves to the side and motions to the woman to come to the window, *pozhaluista*, please. The woman hesitates, then comes forward, but it's all dark beyond, millenary and organic and she can't see anything, not even the rails that erase themselves in the shadows. She presses her forehead to the cold glass and her hands shape a telescope around her eyes, blocking the reflection. She smells of flowers and smoke. Aliocha looks at her—the transparent cartilage of her nose, her ductile profile—and reaches out to tap her on the shoulder. She starts and turns toward him, he points an index finger at his thorax and says, Aliocha. The woman, looking in his eyes for the first time, surprised by the boy's bluntness, places a hand in turn on her chest and says, Hélène.

They share their names, share a light, share cigarettes. She tells him she is French, *frantsouzkaïa,* again with this gesture of a palm against her sternum, leaning on the second syllable, *frantsouzkaïa,* and opposite her, Aliocha nods. French, he's disappointed—although he doesn't know anything about French women, nothing, only has an idea of Fantines, Eugénies and Emmas, obligatory women, fragments of their psyches glimpsed in school textbooks, relegated far in his mind from those who dazzle him, Lady Gaga for example. And this woman, yes, he would have thought she was American, instinctively he would have said she was from Wyoming or Arizona, a woman who's not afraid of wide open spaces and who takes long-distance trains—France is just an itty-bitty country. More smiles, polite. And then they fall silent. Can't say much to each other because without a common language, they don't have anything but these primitive signs, beginnings of a pantomime they manage alright. They've been in these cramped quarters for nearly an hour now, side by side, she holds out her glass, it's vodka, she says, articulating *vodka* exaggeratedly, but he recoils, uncomfortable, shakes his head, *niet, niet,* and then finally yes, takes the glass by its handle—a motion he has never made before in his life, taking a glass by its handle, bringing the thumb and index together—and glugs. It seems at this moment the train speeds up, a slight jolt unbalances them, she's thrown against him and he steadies her, she laughs, not bothered, a French woman indeed, and asks Aliocha where he's headed, insistently pointing out the cardinal directions on the four walls of the compartment. He turns to face the direction the train is heading and in answer lifts an arm towards the front of the train; yes, but where? asks Hélène, *gdie?* He turns his palms up to the ceiling in a sign of powerlessness and his skin turns the color of storm, his jaw tenses, the skin of the cheeks grows hollowed, and Hélène presses, Irkutsk? *Da*, Aliocha answers in suprise, *da*, Irkutsk. That's in nineteen hours, says Hélène, her index swirling once around the face of her watch, and then she writes the number 19 on the window with her finger, nineteen, and they go back to waiting, side by side.

It's now nearly five in the morning and they are still there, Hélène doesn't have anything left to drink in her Snow Queen's hanap, but there are cigarettes still, so they smoke again, we will never know why they remain this way, not speaking, not touching, she should have left long ago—or even, she never should have ventured into this train packed with soldiers, this is no place for you sweetheart, you're looking for trouble, that's what Anton, her Russian lover, would have said, the man she had followed all the way to Siberia, on the banks of the Yenisey and right to the Divnogorsk dam, which he was

40

in charge of now; and, similarly, Aliocha should have gone to sleep, should have anticipated that fleeing the train would take all his strength, or, if he changed his mind, that the training would be exhausting, would slay him.

But they don't move, standing before the pane of glass which is like a movie screen for them, where everything stirs gently, molecular as terror and desire, and then suddenly the night tears open and the landscape hardens outside, clean, geometrical, pure lines and new perspectives, the end of the organic night, the forest rises up in the razing light of dawn and it's still the same forest, the same slender trees, the same orangey trunks, a forest identical to itself to this extent is insane, even if you glimpsed a river welling up beneath the ice, bushes of pale flowers, snow in brownish puddles along the length of a muddy path, rooftops, fences, even then it's still the same forest, on and on, not the ocean but the skin of the Earth, the epidermis of Russia, the claws and the silk, and then in the first rays of dawn their faces are revealed—another event: Hélène is startled to discover that he's so young, a kid, even though he has the build of an athlete, and Aliocha is surprised that she is older than he thought, thirty, thirty-five, maybe double his own age; she is disconcerted by the purplish marks on one side of his face, by his swollen nose and colorless complexion, so livid it's like a corpse—where has his blood gone? and he is struck by her heavy eyelids, beneath which her gaze runs to the edge of the world, light, clear, a river— what kind of eyes are these? They finally step away from each other, Hélène is the first to make a move to leave, placing a hand on the door handle, when Aliocha suddenly grabs her wrist and turns her to face him, she lets out a cry, her flesh retracts, breath cut short, and with her arm held captive, upright, she stammers what, what is it? Everything is happening as though the truce had ended with the night, as though the time when words are something other than shouts had disintegrated, a place where we show ourselves without fear, and as though, catapulted out of this digression, expelled from this sacrarium, they had taken their places once again in the cycle of human violence.

Aliocha lets go at once, confused, red, flushed, his blood racing back, his blood running beneath his skin. He rushes to show that he's sorry, didn't mean to scare her, touches her wrist which she pulls away quickly, turning her head, it's nothing, she heads for the door but he holds her back again by the shoulder, rough, always this force, and now he speaks to her, an astonishing flow of words, trembling of the lips, words that crash into each other and this language that rolls, rolls, pulsing at top speed, a dialect or slang she can't tell, can't catch a single word but the meaning is clear—the boy's face is so intense, so expressive, eyes stretching to his temples, circles gray beneath them—he wants to come with her into her compartment, doesn't want to go back up the train to the third class cars and back to Letchov the sadist and the others in their fatigues and buzz cuts, he wants her to hide him. Understand? Understand? He holds her by the shoulders and shakes her like a plum tree, then takes his military papers out of his back pocket and pretends to tear them up, throws his laminated card on the ground and stomps on it, movements interrupted by worried glances at Hélène who thinks she's understood, you don't want to go, is that it?

The countryside speeds by now through the openings in the gray cell they've occupied together, side by side, two beans in a pod, united in the same jolts, the same moments of acceleration and of slowing down, where they've intertwined the smoke from their cigarettes and the warmth of their breath. Aliocha holds his breath now, he's no beggar, no victim, he's just like her, he's running away, that's all. The woman looks the boy straight in the eye—a clearing opens, very green, in the dirty dawn—and bites her lip. Follow me.

THE FIRST corridor is empty, everyone's fast asleep—it's outside that things are happening, the dawn raising up the forest at full tilt, lifting each trunk to vertical, the bluish underbrush perforated by rays charged with a carnal light, the taiga like a magnetic cloth, modulated to infinity by the new thickness of the air. Hélène, captivated by the outside, lingers insensibly—to pass through the picture window and land in the moss, a tuck and roll and then infiltration—but there's this young man at her heels, breathing down her neck, and she hurries, speeds up again into the next corridor where a silhouette blocks their passage, a middle-aged man, spotless shirt and clean-shaven nape, phone to his ear, eyes wandering, Hélène brakes at the last minute, in her rush nearly barreling into him, *pozhaluista*, she says as she passes, the guy flattens himself against the wall, freeing a passage and slowly turns his head to follow these two with his eyes, these two coming from the other end of the train, the foreigner and the conscript, one behind the other but visibly together—another Westerner come to eye up the backwoods of Russia, he would have liked to put a hand on her ass if the kid wasn't there, his eyes cast down but his build sturdy, you can see it right away. Train car follows train car, the same doors with warm, sticky handles, the heavy panels sheathed in black rubber that must be unstuck one from the other spreading elbows out to horizontal, the same accordion-pleated vestibules that shake, where the temperature drops, where the ground whips past through gaps in the metallic floor—wood ties, gravel, patches of grass—the deserted corridors like gaping holes that snatch at them and they throw themselves in headfirst eyes riveted to the ground, they must not stop, they must do it fast, and then they're at Hélène's compartment.

The door slides open quickly, here, they go inside. Hélène collapses onto a bench and Aliocha stays standing, doesn't know where to put himself, sizes up the place. It's quiet here. It smells good. Or maybe it just doesn't smell like anything, not feet nor mouths nor unwashed skin, it just smells clean and like the foreigner's things. It's first class for sure, but not super luxurious, thinks Aliocha, looking around, not over-the-top—he makes a mental note to tell the others who imagine thick white bathrobes, thick carpet, minibar and champagne—there's a large window where, in order to clear the view completely, Hélène took down the curtains and the metal rod as soon as she got here, two large facing mirrors that multiply space to infinity, two bunks with mattresses, white sheets, white pillow, white duvet, the pleasure of a fresh bed. Hélène clears off the things she'd put on one of the bunks and indicates to Aliocha

47

standing in the middle of the compartment, you can sit down, there's no one else here. A bag of snacks is on the small table, Hélène pulls out a bottle and holds it towards Aliocha, want some? He refuses, still standing, his shaved head and military clothes clash here, lie down, you can sleep, she points to the bunk, Aliocha sits on the edge, undoes the first buttons of his shirt but thinks twice, doesn't take it off, decides to keep his shoes on too. After a moment he drops onto his side and with his knees bent and arms crossed over his chest, he falls asleep.

Hélène stays awake. The day is bright now. Still the same slow and massive unfurling of the countryside, still the same quiet stride of the train, sixty kilometers an hour is an ideal speed to watch the mountains rise, those mountains that disturb the landscape now, decisive slopes lined with dark conifers that hurtle towards the rails, the realm of bears. At the end of a tunnel, the craggy relief engulfs the window and obscures the sky whole, leaving it to the traveler to invent the most plausible or the most wild off-camera scene, but Hélène doesn't need to invent anything, everything is happening here, right here in front of her: all she has to do is look at the soldier sleeping on the bunk to feel that his presence is absurd, out of place, and to see that something's off here, something's short-circuiting. In the end, whether it was this young man or a bear stretched out there, it would amount to the same thing, the same enormity, as though the real was suddenly crumbling, subverted by powerful dreams or completely other substances capable of catalyzing metamorphoses, as though the real was tearing apart under the pressure of a faint but immutable deviation, something far bigger, far stronger than it—but no, there are no dreams in Hélène's head, no drugs in her blood, the young man is well and truly there—indeed, *he* is the real, the tangible present moment of life, here, breathing with his mouth open a little, body rising and falling imperceptibly with each breath, and if she were to place a hand on him, on his pale and downy cheek, on his shoulder, she knows she would feel him alive, he would stir, open an eye and wake up. Hélène smiles. She agreed to take Aliocha in without hesitation, without even really weighing his request, and whether suspect ease or absence of discernment it doesn't much matter, she felt overwhelmed by this young man, absolutely unique in the world in the face of his request, and she who had reserved both bunks in the compartment so she might be alone with an opening onto Siberia to remember and imagine—two ways of seeing clearly— she had welcomed this stranger. She turns her eyes and lets them drift outside: what's done is done.

She's thirsty. They smoked too much last night. She takes her glass and goes out to get some hot water from the samovar, hydrological gem located at the end of the corridor across from the *provodnitsa's* quarters—in this car, a small, dark-haired woman with rounded arms and olive skin, lips painted with fuchsia lipstick, bright eyed and bushy tailed even in the early morning. Hélène greets her, takes a tea bag and pours hot water into her glass, the two women smile at each other, then Hélène points to the landscape in motion and, for the sake of conversation, asks if there are bears here: *medved? medved?* The attendant looks surprised and then grows animated, *da, da,* of course there are, turns to go back into her compartment, comes out again cheerfully carrying a digital camera, and soon images are scrolling past on the tiny screen, the Siberian forest, dark conifers with red trunks, spruce, aspen, a mess of larch, mountains, more villages created by the railway, and suddenly the shape of a bear beside a stream, there it is, beneath thin bright poplars, big brown teddy on all fours, the short-sighted look of heavy mammals, still there in the next photo but standing on its hind paws and terrible now, the moist pale pink of its mouth caught in the lens, its close-set eyes, black, hard, mica, and the same animal is in the third photo as well, the back of it this time, half hidden in the brambles, in the wild.

Back at the compartment—she jumps when she opens the door, Aliocha's decidedly insoluble body lying there like that on the bunk—Hélène corners herself against the window, presses her head against it and wanders, takes the tracks backwards the way we head back in time, to two days earlier in Krasnoyarsk while she was waiting for Anton in a parking lot beside the dam, the windshield of the car fogged up on the inside by her own carbon dioxide and clouded on the outside by the thousands of microscopic droplets ripped from the mist and projected against her car. She can't see anything and so she gets out, choosing the drizzle over remaining shut away inside the car, blind. There, more than the spectacle of the falls (seeing them, Hélène thinks back to scenes from Westerns: the heroes stuffed inside barrels that are dropped into the water, the silent crowd holding its breath, the barrel that gives out and the dismembered body tossed in the hydraulic frenzy, or else the guy who emerges intact from the barrel, stunned, bashed about, fingers brandished in a V for victory) it was their hum, the aural power of the waterfalls that had hypnotized her, and she didn't hear her lover coming up behind her and placing a hand flat on the back of her neck; worse, she barely felt the kiss he breathed behind her ear. Oh Hélène. She finally turned around, laughing, you're here! But he was already probing her with his eyes, quiet.

That day, she had escaped in the car along the Yenisey, venturing into the villages built along the river. Wooden piers stretched out into the green water and she imagined summertime and swims, the leaps of kids. Old roads ran alongside log houses with delicately wrought wooden shutters, with windows veiled in lace, with flowerpots neatly aligned, with gardens well-tended. She attempted a conversation in sign language with an old woman wearing heavy black skirts who stood behind her painted wooden fence—the top of each plank cut into a diamond for more elegance—and the woman ended up coming out, thinking Hélène was lost. She never stopped smiling—her few remaining teeth were gold— and at the end she sang a song for Hélène, her utterly steady voice mastering a heart-wrenching melody while her round foot kept time against the ground. Hélène listened, frozen, and then suddenly, stupidly, she thought she should pay her, and since she didn't have a single ruble on her, she had run to her car which, of course, wouldn't start, a problem with the starter, she let out a curse between her teeth, damn it, damn it, start, and turned the key again but nothing happened, and the old woman had lots of time to scamper to the back of the garden and come back to the car with a bag of berries in her hand, her smile even larger, frightening in her friendliness, Hélène had nodded and pretended not to understand and then, when the motor finally started, she had sped away, full of shame.

Anton's black eyes wouldn't let her go. So, how was the day? Hélène spoke of the incredible Russians, the tree-lined hills around the village, beautiful though cold still, and the Yenisey which, yes, was certainly the most majestic river in Russia. He listened, tense, keen, knew every dip and swell of the turbulence that agitated her, an effervescence no less strong, no less exceptional than the one shattering the atmosphere a few hundred meters behind them, listened to her with such attention that he ended up hearing everything she didn't say, how difficult it was for her living here, out of place, out of her own climate, her language, blind and deaf she would say over and over, laughing, and alone—this is Siberian life, he joked in the first days, life in a world turned inside out like a glove, raw, wild, empty, you'll see, you'll get used to it! But on that day at the dam, he could see that she was fighting, searching for something to hold on to, devouring him with her eyes as though she didn't recognize him. And in truth, things had changed: he was now master of the dam, heir to the Soviet industrial epic, and she knew he was proud even if he spoke ironically, lightly, about this reversal of fortune—his being elected to manage the hydropower plant in Divnogorsk, a fabulous promotion, which sealed his return to Russia, he who had been born into the kitchens of dissent and just as quickly whisked away, wrapped in a flowered shawl with a long black fringe, pressed tightly against his mother. He kissed the inside of Hélène's wrist, they loved each other like crazy, she couldn't possibly leave.

And then she left. She had to act fast, and brutally, distance herself from him as though she were pushing him away with a stick, like a dog. The next day, after following the black car with her eyes until it disappeared, the car that came each day at eight o'clock to take him to the dam, she knew she would go. That morning, wearing his most gorgeous suit, he had sung to her in the kitchen, had mimed the flummeries he would have to perform in a few hours before the delegation from Moscow, mimicking the large bellies, the short necks and the triple chins, he had made her laugh, twisting his face into dripping smiles, preparing clumsy compliments, ceremonial poems and sensationalist tributes which he uttered while juggling spoons and sprinkling his sunny-side-up eggs with paprika, he was funny and insolent, his vivacity unparalleled, he was magnificent. Once the heavy sedan of *apparatchiks* had disappeared—he made his chain bracelet tinkle and played with his black sunglasses to signal to Hélène, I won't be truly respected until they change my company car, a big Porsche Cayenne, that's what we'll ask for, ok darling?—once it had made the turn at the end of the road, Hélène's hand, which a few seconds earlier had been sending kisses to Anton, froze in the air, fell alongside her thigh, and she looked for something to lean against, her legs weak. Then the street, the village and Siberia had redrawn their maleficent circle around her. She dragged herself to their bed and lay back down. Thought she might spend two days sleeping and waiting until he came back. Then nothing. An empty day. Evening was falling when she got dressed, packed her bag in a rush, and headed to the Krasnoyarsk station. The first train was due at 10 pm. The Trans-Siberian. The mythic railway line. Two iron lines of flight that would take her all the way to the Pacific. The path of freedom that opened onto the ocean. She paid for her ticket in cash without a moment's hesitation and looked for a place to wait—she didn't want a false start, didn't want to go back home until the time of the train—sat down in a nondescript café near the station, flipping through magazines she didn't understand. The final hour was the hardest, when everything was closed, and she ended up freezing on a bench beside the platform, ignoring the calls from Anton that lit up her phone. And then the train.

A steep-sided valley, walls of stark gray rock close in tightly around the train, the window darkens, and Hélène's face is reflected there, dilating, carving out a passage to events of the past—they met in Paris the winter before, Anton was born in Moscow, far behind the Iron Curtain, his family in exile, the sounds of Russian boil inside his French, he's the son of Gogol and Stalin, the shivering child who waited on Christmas night for the brightly colored troika and the long-lashed reindeer, and who in the morning found instead Mishka the little bear in his lousy shoe. He is Andreï Rublev and Marina Tsvetaeva, he is Yuri Gagarin, he is Tchaikovsky, he is Trotsky himself, his name is Anton Chekhov. She has a tragic and patchy image of Russia, a jumbled montage involving the fatal fall of a baby carriage down a monumental staircase in Odessa, the firebrand in the eyes of Michel Strogoff, the gymnast Elena Mukhina spinning on the uneven bars, the fevered face of Lenin as he addresses the crowd, the Soviet Union flag at the top of the Reichstag, doctored photos, Brezhnev's eyebrows and Solzhenitsyn's beard, *La Mouette* at the Odéon cinema one spring night, thousands of prisoners digging a canal between the Baltic and the White Sea, Nureyev leaping across the border in an airport, a parade of tanks on the Red Square and decorated tunics glimpsed between flakes of snow, the *dusha*, the invasion of Afghanistan in December 1979, queues in front of stores seen on the news, large women swathed in scarves, the Sakharovs back to Moscow after years of internal exile in Gorki, spies traded on bridges at night, the birthmark on Gorbachev's forehead, Soyuz, Yeltsin drunk, the smile of a young billionaire as he buys the Chelsea Football Club, top models, the mafia, murders, the hold-up of the entire country, the Chechen nightmare, Putin's face, the lobby of the building where Anna Politkovskaya lived, the verdigris skin tone of Viktor Yushchenko, the war again, Ossetia and Georgia, the family of old believers found on the taiga after seventy years; she has never seen the Red Square, the bulbous domes of Saint Basil's Cathedral or the frozen Volga, doesn't speak a word of Russian, but she's read *Anna Karenina* three times, hums the melody of *Doctor Zhivago* and still knows the taiga, the tundra, and the steppe by heart, geography-textbook definitions which she recites to him word for word. They are in love. At first she loves the fact that he is free, that Russia disgusts him, that he has neither nostalgia nor remorse. In January, he leaves for Krasnoyarsk, she goes with him, and from the moment of their arrival at the airport she's touched to see him back here, to hear him speaking his own language, gestures suddenly expansive, voice wider. Would she have even spoken to him if he hadn't been the man from the forbidden country? Would she have even loved him if there hadn't been, at the heart of all this, Russia— this country she is now fleeing?

The young man sleeps on in front of her, less than a meter away. His shirt and t-shirt, untucked, leave bare an area of very white skin, hip and belly smooth, bones jutting and abdomen hollow below the completely hairless chest. She glimpses a tattoo just above the groin, something faded, a woman's face and Cyrillic letters, the Virgin perhaps, maybe a prayer, and now, thrown into an archaeology of traces, she notices the bitten nails edged with torn dead skin, the ashy fuzz above the upper lip, the little scars on the inner arms, the chain around the neck and the medallion pendant. Bit by bit, she gets used to this strange being, here, absorbs its impact, its mass and internal temperature, the slowed-down flow of blood, the flexing of the muscles, the rough fabric of the fatigues and the cheap cotton of the military clothes, the black leather belt, and finally touches the invisible stratigraphy that composes all bodies, all movements, all feelings: this young soldier also embodies the entire country, he's an archive of all the Russian wars—"the homeland our mother, the war our stepmother," Anton had taught her this adage one night when they'd drunk iced vodka and smoked hash on the roof of a building on the boulevard Raspail, and then he had concluded, irresistible, index finger drilling into his temple, you see what I mean about that crazy country? Bunch of nutcases. Hélène draws back instinctively, reminds herself that this is also a body at her mercy.

A KNOCK AT the door. Hélène jumps—daydreams and games of memory over, she rushes to Aliocha and wakes him with a finger to his lips, then to her own, shh! Listen. The silence petrifies them together inside the compartment. More knocks at the door—sharp little blows, inquisitive—Aliocha leaps to his feet, panicked, Hélène answers *da, da* in a sleepy voice, shuffles some papers, scatters a few newspapers over the ground, opens her laptop, rummages in her bags, letting them think the agitation in here is of someone being disturbed, interrupted at work, while with a tilt of her head she indicates a cavity above the door: a space for oversized luggage that she hasn't used (she'd

65

just shoved her bags under the bench with her foot), she points it out to Aliocha who understands immediately and pulls himself up into the recess with the strength of his arms, sliding in headfirst, shrinking himself into fetal position. He's quick but they're getting impatient on the other side of the door, knock-knock, Hélène has pulled on a t-shirt, she rumples her pillow, and finally turns to reach a hand toward the door handle, lifts her head one last time: Aliocha's knee is sticking out past the door frame but she has to do it now. She opens the door. Two *provodnitsys*, the one from her car—the dark-haired dark-skinned one whose fuchsia lipstick had faded—and the other, the blonde, from the third-class car, fat-thighed Letchov's car. Aliocha's car. Yes? The two women don't speak French, their hands flutter in the air like moths, the blonde especially is spewing words and Hélène doesn't understand a thing but decides that pre-empting any suspicions without seeming to submit to a search is the best course, and so as though by accident, as though it were a result of a sudden jolt of the train, she slides the door open wider, and the two women immediately check inside, the blonde bumping into the dark-haired one and sticking her head through the door—Hélène tenses, the veins in her neck rise beneath the skin, imperceptible, an electric charge, she's terrified that the top of the blonde attendant's head where her crimped hair puffs up will touch Aliocha's knee; or that the boy's smell, strong, but which she herself has stopped smelling after all these hours spent together, will alert them, will signal his passage through this compartment—or worse, his presence—any second now they'll touch, the top of the head grazing the knee, a disaster.

The attendant forces a smile but doesn't step past the doorway, contents herself with scouring the compartment with her eyes, including the lower part around the bunks, as though she were searching for something completely other than a man, letting her eyes trail over the foreigner's things, her mess of boots, her clothes visible inside the open bag, her beauty products, her perfume bottle, and then she finally steps back, making little motions with her hands that might signify I'm sorry, and walks away disappointed. The other attendant takes Hélène's hands and squeezes them with a benevolent smile, Hélène shakes her head, it's nothing, nothing at all, then she slides the door closed, clack, and falls backwards onto the bunk, heavy as a suitcase. Raises her eyes to Aliocha and signals for him to wait a little longer, to keep silent.

Later, they sit facing each other, exhausted, and although she fights to resist—after all, she doesn't know this guy, he might go through her things, might steal them or worse—might attack her in her sleep (he did threaten her earlier, didn't he?)—Hélène falls asleep in front of Aliocha, who's taken aback, and suddenly stands guard.

He keeps his face turned away at first so as not to

see her. Not because he's scared of her—she's not big enough to give him any trouble, one smack would be enough—but he has no way to anticipate her movements, her reactions: she's a Westerner, and he doesn't spend time with Westerners, doesn't know how they work. The only thing he knows is that the moment the two women knocked on the door, Hélène stepped over into his camp. In the second when she opened the door to let them see that she was indeed alone—in that second she became his accomplice. She may not even know why she did it, maybe just for fun, to play the game. But she didn't act under duress, he's sure of it: she's a different story, he doesn't know what, but it's something else.

She lies stretched out in front of him on her side, lids still smudged with yesterday's eyeshadow, mascara dry at the ends of her lashes, rumpled shirt, black nails. How far is she going? Two bunks for her alone, the whole compartment to spread out, how much would this madness cost? He doesn't dare get up to rummage through them but notices a few papers on the table, reaches out an arm like a pincer, touches the pile from a distance, among them a train ticket—he recognizes the rectangular cardboard, thicker than the other papers— picks it up, and with some difficulty makes out the boxes filled in with codes mixing numbers and Cyrillic, capital letters, small letters. Twenty-seven thousand two hundred and twenty rubles. He slowly re-reads the number. His saliva tastes of burning metal. He makes out the destination. Vladivostok. That's where she's going. That's at the other end of the country, in the east, he knows this much, there's ocean there, a naval base where the country's fleet is anchored in secret, light gray buildings reeking of machine oil, undetectable submarines with unknown destinations, just like him. What's she going to do there? The only thing he knows is that now there's something they share.

In a few hours they'll reach Irkutsk and that's where he will get off. Lots of people board the Trans-Siberian just for that: to get off at Irkutsk and head to Lake Baikal. In the train car, the other passengers talk of nothing but this, to see Baikal, to finally see Baikal. Aliocha has never seen it, only knows the name, three shards of quartz tossed into the sun, and he pronounces it quietly, as the night and Irkutsk draw nearer: Baikal! Magic formula and secret code: little by little, as though she had sprung up from the forest that rushes against the windowpane, a young woman appears, same age as him, slender arms and mermaid hair, amber cheekbones and crazy-big eyes that eat up her face, blue eyes of an astonishing depth— the night he slept with her, he murmured the only compliment he's ever given a woman, your eyes are like Lake Baikal, and she smiled, pressing herself against him, she'd never seen the lake either—and Aliocha thinks back to that last morning: a man in an overcoat came to get her, they left the building around ten o'clock, he

71

sees again the snowed-in courtyard, the white car, and the girl, *chapka* pulled down to her eyebrows, walking with her head held high and back straight, a rough hand pushing her along; the scene unspools sharp and in real time, as though the railway and memory were built upon each other, as though the movement of the train recreated the Baikal-girl in the red wool coat, hands gloved in black, she passes through the screen of glass that carries her away forever, and just before the turn, that fugitive movement through the rear window: a brief look back with fingers outstretched.

A little before Irkutsk, Hélène wakes up. Seeing Aliocha slouched there, lost in thought and occupying, it seems to her, an increased volume of space, she grows irritated. Tells herself it's time he got out of here. She's tired of it now: he's taking up so much room. Big feet, big hands, big legs, his torso only as thick as a playing card but the impression that he's opening out like a folding ruler every time he moves. Both of them all the way to Vladivostok—in other words three days and three nights in the train—it's unplayable. He has to get off at Irkutsk and figure it out for himself. How long has she been asleep? It's five o'clock. She sits up on her bunk. Irkutsk! Taps the screen of her watch and lifts a thumb to Aliocha who sits up as well: Irkutsk, in an hour! He jumps. His heart picks up speed. Irkutsk, he's got to get ready. He looks down and considers his clothes, this isn't going to work, these fatigues, this khaki t-shirt, it won't work, he needs something else to wear, does Hélène have anything? Again, sign language and the facial expressions that go along with it as he pronounces Russian words exaggeratedly, quietly, words Hélène doesn't understand and so he pulls at his pants, pulls at his t-shirt, then points to Hélène's shirt, give it to me. She understands but takes offense, that's enough, stop being ridiculous, frowns while her index tick-tocks from left to right, a metronome, *niet*, not the shirt, not Anton's shirt. Aliocha

73

tightens his lips, face closed, pushes himself down more firmly on the seat, it's very clear to him that this woman has discarded him, that she's no longer his accomplice, even though he kept so quiet and made himself so small in her compartment, he doesn't get it, digs in his heels and pushes a finger into Hélène's chest, presses it against her sternum and his voice grows threatening, the shirt, hand it over, the shirt, come on! The tension rises all at once, and Hélène glares at him without batting an eye. OK. It was too good. Aliocha stares back, their eyes lock, ready to charge. The shirt, the goddamn shirt, give it. His voice trembles at the end of the syllables: he won't go so far as to take it from her, she knows it, and he knows it too, this is the very thing that enrages him. He takes a step closer and pushes her, once, twice, until Hélène falls back onto her bunk. Give me the shirt. She's paralyzed—she can't believe what's happening. Turn around, she signs to him to turn towards the door, turn around. Grabs a t-shirt from her suitcase, unbuttons her shirt, puts the t-shirt on, it's anger more than fear that overwhelms her, let him take what he wants and get out of here. Aliocha stares at the door, catches his breath, arms crossed over his chest: he's demanding this shirt because it means his freedom, it means his life. I don't have a choice. Hélène holds out the shirt with her face averted, sharp movement and lips closed, he pulls it on carefully, his fingers pass over the buttonholes, one by one lining up the panels of the shirt, it's a soft cotton, blueish white decorated with pearl buttons, a creasing she knows well. Once she's dressed again Hélène sits heavily onto the seat and opens a book—it's over. But a moment later, looking up to see Aliocha in Anton's shirt, she's unnerved: she would never have thought a shirt could transform the kid to this extent—not just disguise him, but change his whole aura.

Aliocha discovers himself in the mirror. He, too, has a hand over his mouth and his eyes are wide, stunned, he can't turn away from the image; something obscure holds him there, his breathing changes tempo, grows slower, Hélène is sure she can hear it, sure she can see his spine gently straightening; the shirt softens his long silhouette, his body lean and knotted as though beaten dry with a stick, tattooed with bad ink, and causes a free man to appear—a djinn emerges from the magic cloth. He'll need to change his pants, too, think Hélène, the fatigues wreck the whole thing, and now she's the one who rummages through her suitcase, pulls out a pair of pale blue jeans and hands them to the boy, go on, put these on. Aliocha swallows his saliva and takes off the fatigues—he has long pallid thighs covered in bruises, some of them turning yellow—and pulls on the pants. The width is good but the length—on Aliocha, Hélène's jeans, even though she could never be called short, become pirate pants, only reaching to mid-calf. It doesn't matter—anything's better than the damn camouflage. Hélène nods, looking at him standing there now, about to leave. And then she picks up her bright

76

purple scarf, the one that marked her out a few hours ago in the Krasnoyarsk station, wraps it firmly around his neck—for an instant, she almost reaches to pat his shoulders, smooth the fabric with little feminine gestures, arrange it suitably. Hurry the goodbyes, don't dwell on them, quick, quick, Aliocha takes her hand and leaning forward as always he murmurs rapidly *spassiba, spassiba*, Hélène shakes her head, it's nothing, it's nothing, pulls her hand back, relieved to be leaving and even more relieved that he's leaving, that this whole thing is ending, ready to look back with a knot in her stomach on this sordid scenario where she gave herself the lucky draw, proclaimed herself the hero, the stranger who falls from the sky, saves you and then slips away, ready to rack up self-convincing statements—I did my utmost, I did all that I could—all the while knowing she's incapable of believing it: the worm of guilt is already lodging itself in her gut.

They have to separate. She'll go out first. They can't

be seen together when the train enters the station in Irkutsk, she has to divert attention. Seeing her getting ready, he feels a wave of panic. I'm going to go to the restaurant car, she whispers, I'll make sure the *provodnitsys* see me and at Irkutsk—hup, off you go! She picks up her bag, slides the door open and then turns back one last time, *bonne chance* Aliocha—the too-short pants, the big boots alone that could betray him, the fine cotton shirt, Hélène's scarf—he looks like a determined kid, tight fists shoved into his pockets—a last smile bursting with courage for him, a last glance that goes along with it like a push, and in the doorway she calls back, remember, Irkutsk, twenty minutes—again the watch and two hands lifted with fingers spread, twice in a row, and turning her back on her shame, she plunges down the corridor.

Head back up the train cars all the way to the restaurant, pass the *provodnitsa's* compartment where she's reading inside (she startles when she sees Hélène charging along at full speed, bag over her shoulder), pass through the second class cars whose doors are all ajar, cast an eye inside the compartments where no one is sleeping, where people are still eating, containers of *pirojki* picked up in a previous station, cold milk, tomato juice in cartons, apples, forest berries, cookies; where people are drinking—vodka, always—where everyone's waiting for Irkutsk, the last stop before night falls; head straight through the third class cars, step over knees, duck under arms, dodge the kids playing in the middle of the floor, avoid the wandering hands of drunk soldiers—Hélène is oblivious to the fact, as she passes the boy's bunk, that Sergeant Letchov still hasn't noticed his absence, in a crazy rage with his young mistress, a woman he terrorizes—he has her followed by guys who owe him everything, in particular owe him for having escaped military service—and next Hélène is spotted by the blond *provodnitsa* who's vigorously tying a big garbage bag, a brief nod with a pointed look—similarly, Hélène is oblivious to the fact that this woman is not fooled, she knows Aliocha is hiding on the train.

And then the restaurant car, like a bright lantern between two dim passenger cars, with heavy doors that open onto the antiquated décor—wood-paneled walls, four-person tables, printed tablecloths, benches where people press in shoulder to shoulder, little tin spoons, luncheonette dishes—while outside they're already in the suburbs of Irkutsk, more wooden houses with carved shutters, more impeccable little gardens, nature elbowed out of the way and buildings crowded in to form cities, rows of dwellings rising higher and higher, a few tall towers.

It's still early, two men sharing a plate of salami are the only other diners in here, the others will come later. A little pot of *lapcha* is placed before Hélène, chicken noodle soup, and at this exact moment the train comes to a halt in the Irkutsk station and the phone screen lights up with Anton's name. A message in her voice-mail: Hélène—the texture of the voice so clear she trembles—if you took the train in Krasnoyarsk last night, as my friends—my *sbires* as you say—tell me, you must be near Irkutsk by this time and, strangely, I like knowing you are in that city—the "a" dark and deep, nearly a closed "o," the warm vibration of the "r," rolled in the base of his throat; my love, soon you will see Baikal, make sure you leave the door of the compartment open, you can see the lake from the corridor for a full half hour, make sure you don't miss it, it's a treasure for the Russians, the country's pearl, but for me, for us, the men of Siberia, it's simply the sea—the labials that linger, the dentals that collide, the light hiss of saliva under the upper lip—yes, I said "us, the men of Siberia," I'm rediscovering my country, Hélène, and I am happy; last night I sang karaoke with the *apparatchiks* of society, the Moscovites with their big bellies, fierce guys, and there was a woman there with us who sang that old Cossack

81

song I love, *Oï, to ne vetcher,* and I cried—a silence, she makes out the rush of self-control when vulnerability threatens; Hélène, call me when you get to Vladivostok, we'll find a way, goodbye darling—and it feels as though she could reach out a hand and touch his face. Hélène turns to the window. Irkutsk. Anton is a sorcerer.

The platform outside is packed. The conscripts stand massed together. Hélène, who hadn't paid them much attention in Krasnoyarsk, can see nothing but them now. Where are they going? What will they be doing? They're right there, on the other side of the glass—throngs of them, all these young men reeling, sending messages to their mothers, their girlfriends, saying they don't know when the first leave will be, saying they're worried about their dogs. She examines each face—her way of parceling out the group, allowing individuals to emerge, Nikolaïs, Sachas, Constantins, Dimitris, Sergueïs. Young men who seem to form a unit, but who in fact are only clinging to each other for dear life.

Hélène shivers: Aliocha got out, he must be thread-
ing through the crowd at this very moment, plausible
silhouette of a young student headed for the shores of
Baikal where he'll paint watercolors, compose poems,
unless he happens to be one of the young trail-clearing
volunteers enlisted by environmental activists of the
GBT (Great Baikal Trail). He'll have that determined
gait and chest always inclined forward, he'll make it.
The soup grows cold in the small pot. Hélène, nervous,
stirs her spoon in it slowly without managing to swallow
a bite, plunges her eyes to the bottom of the earthen-
ware vessel, she must not look outside. The thirty minutes of this stop seem to take hours. The train starts up
again without any whistle blowing or gathering of the
conscripts on the platform for a roll call, Aliocha snuck
out and no one saw anything, she glues her face to the
window hoping to catch the tall shape of the one who's
escaping with her scarf around his neck, inspects the
platforms, the back sides of buildings, and further off

the mountains, the fences, he got away, he did it. Hélène orders a vodka: she will drink to Aliocha's health. She's alone, she lingers, and here's that song that lingers in her memory now too, *Oi, to ne vecher*, the song she heard last Christmas at a party with some of Anton's Russian friends, who also grew up in dissidence. She doesn't remember how, but somewhere in the middle of the night twenty of them were suddenly singing together, improvising a polyphonic choir, vodka enhancing their ardor and lyricism without ruining the melody. Anton had taken her aside and held her by the shoulders to translate the song: it's the story of a Russian peasant who dreams one night that his horse tramples him and that a wind from the east tears his hat off his head—Anton's face was close to hers, in a state of exaltation that would have made any other woman run, but she had been deeply moved, he was drunk but still in the space of euphoria, the place where we are both strongest and most lucid—the next day the peasant goes to tell his dream to the ataman, the ruler of the Cossacks, who predicts the Tsar will have him beheaded, and that's exactly what happens: the man would later lead the peasant's revolt, be taken prisoner and decapitated. The plains, horses, violence: a typically Russian story, Anton had concluded, pouring himself another drink.

Hélène empties her glass in one movement, turns her head, she's alone now in the restaurant car, the two men from the next table have vanished and the waitress comes over and says, in English: Baikal! Baikal, ten minutes!—she raises her ten fingers spread wide and makes a motion for Hélène to leave, lunch service is on hold. Hélène gets up and retraces the long path through the train, recognizes faces and nods, smiles again at the *provodnitsys*, and when she reaches the door of her compartment, Baikal appears. There it is, far off, on the corridor side. Fragmentary at first, a liquid ribbon glimpsed between two hillsides, then suddenly immense and violet, running alongside the length of the train.

85

People shout out—Baikal! Baikal!—and the passengers hurry out of compartments in a beautiful synchronized movement. Hélène opens hers to toss her bag inside and can't stifle a cry: Aliocha is there.

She closes the door again violently without going in, without even meeting the boy's eyes, pivots toward the spectacle of the lake with her back pressed against the door. He didn't get off, damn it! On either side of her, in a mess of multi-pocketed bags and zippers, people have pulled out cameras and video cameras galore, cell phones held out any which way to try and capture the infinite lake, the gently sloping shores, the deserted holiday hamlets, the log huts, the shore so close and not the slightest wave, barely a lapping, people snap everything they can while the lake remains in sight, stretched out, silky, smooth, sky mirror, not a wrinkle, only a solitary boat barely moving as evening falls, while inside the Trans-Siberian, in the corridors of the first class cars, it's the clamor of a fairground. People shout,

86

sing, share cakes, break down in tears, bottles of vodka are opened and passed down the line, a woman faints from emotion, another recites a poem, a couple dances, everyone is talking at once, and in the general euphoria Hélène forgets about Aliocha confined behind her and melts into the unintelligible commotion, imagining the superlative praises, the lyrical witticisms, the contest of hyperboles—an old man at the end of the car beats his chest and shouts, we Russians may be poor, but we have Baikal! The largest supply of freshwater on Earth! Someone asks loudly, how cold is it, ten, twelve degrees? I don't care, I'd give anything to dive in, replies a woman who is asked to kindly consider the fragile ecosystem. Fascinated, an eight-year-old boy wants to know if the lake contains prehistoric monsters, and someone knowledgeable answers, invertebrates and micro-organisms from the beginning of time. The lake is alternately the inland sea and the sky inversed, the chasm and the sanctuary, the abyss and purity, tabernacle and diamond, it

87

is the blue eye of the Earth, the beauty of the world, and soon, swaying in unison with the other passengers, Hélène, too, is taking a photo with her phone, an image she sends to Anton straightaway, the train is passing Lake Baikal and I am at the window on the corridor side, I'm thinking of you.

The tracks skirt the southern edge of the lake, run northeast now along the other shore, crossing the Selenga delta—domain of the black stork—aquatic fan unfolding over more than a hundred thousand hectares, a labyrinth formed of islands, peninsulas, small lakes and channels, and then they head eastward, a sharp turn, and Lake Baikal disappears. The excitement drops all at once, the volume too, a general subsiding to match the nightfall, and Aliocha's face resurges all in a flash—a boomerang. Hélène whips around and enters the compartment brusquely. Yes, there he is, wedged in. Gripping a pack of cigarettes, he turns an imploring face towards her, wishes he could explain what happened in Irkutsk. It's hard for Hélène to look at him, she wants to go to sleep, to not think of anything anymore. He irritates her, whimpering like this, disguised, ridiculous. She signals for him to be quiet and prepares her bed in large overt movements, lowers the curtain and slips beneath the sheet, hoping the very particular sleep of rail travel will carry her as far away as possible.

She doesn't know that Aliocha *did* get out in Irkutsk. On the platform, beside the train door, someone was selling *omoul* eggs in transparent containers—their orange color gleaming through the plastic box as though the eggs were living matter, as though they were milling around inside their see-through box—the situation was opportune, haggling was in full force, no one was interested in Aliocha who walked around the mass of people and headed straight to the stairwell leading up to a walkway above the platforms. This is where he made his mistake: thinking he was heading towards the station and the streets of the city, he went the opposite way, which led to the furthest train platforms, and a dead end. He was alone and his shirt must have shone slightly phosphorescent—a guard called out to him, Hey you, what are you doing? That area's out of use, no trains! Aliocha stopped dead, then turned to head back, smiling, calm, without trying anything. Since he didn't have a bag, it seemed impossible for him to be a traveler approaching or leaving the train, the guard must not have even asked himself the question, just pointed to the Trans-Siberian, you should board, you'll miss the train. And so Aliocha slipped back in among the first-class passengers, their arms full of vodka and *omoul.*

Hélène sleeps on in front of him. She hasn't left the compartment since Krasnoyarsk aside from the trip to the restaurant car. She had probably planned to brush her teeth, to wash and get ready for bed after Baikal's passage, but he was there, back again, this total loser,

this unpleasant surprise, and his presence had dis-
suaded her from going back out. She doesn't want to
leave me alone in her compartment, is she scared of me
or something? She doesn't trust me—Aliocha examines
her intently—she's helping me, yes, but she doesn't trust
me—he stares at her profile lit by the night light, the
recesses and the grain of her skin, the well-shaped curls
around her earlobe—now she's the captive. How long
have they been together? How many days has he been
on this train? Aliocha concentrates hard to locate a few
temporal reference points—the first roll call at dawn on
the platform in the Yaroslavski station, the shock of the
infinite plain seen for the first time, space so scooped
out he grew dizzy, then the Volga after Nijni Novgorod,
the fight, the first attempt to run away, the meeting with
the foreigner, the second attempt at Irkutsk—but fails to
restore the sequence of nights and days since Moscow,
fails to identify what the date is today.

He lifts a corner of the curtain and casts a glance out

the window, corridor side. Outside, it's still the same chrome-plated night and the train that rolls unerringly, crossing time zones one by one, breaking up time as it charges through space; the train that compacts or dilates the hours, concretes the minutes, stretches out the seconds, continues on pegged to the earth and yet out of sync with earth's clocks: the train like a spaceship. The boy gets up and turns to the mirror above Hélène. The darkness grants him only a shadow puppet, shoulders to head. He goes closer, wonders what his face will look like when he gets home, if anyone will recognize him. And them—will they have white hair and wrinkled skin like in sci-fi movies where the hero returns to his family on Earth after a long cosmic wander? Does railway time match earthly time, the age of his grandmother and the luxuriance of the coming summer, will it carry him to the Baikal-woman in the red coat? Aliocha stays standing in the dark, a delicate balance, his body no more than a vibratile material oscillating in the unplaceable space of the train, he gets dizzy, nearly falls onto Hélène, pulls himself back at the last second, he needs to eat, needs to find something to drink, needs to go out to piss, too, to splash some water on his face, necessary actions that remind him he has a body and this body needs to get the hell off this train.

Staggering, he takes three steps over to the table and crouches down, finds the plastic bag, takes out the bread, stuffs a chicken leg into a pocket of his jeans, a handful of berries, and sits down in the corner of the compartment. The noise he makes when he bites into the bread explodes in his ear, frightening—he'll wake her—he swallows slowly, hasn't eaten anything since Novossibirsk and his throat hurts; next the chicken which he forces himself to eat just as slowly, and finally the berries, growing warm in the hollow of his hand. Feeling around then in the darkness, sliding the door open noiselessly and ejecting himself, hurtling down the car in long strides without becoming blinded by the whiskey light that stings the eyes—everything is happening as though the influx of sugar in his blood is propelling him forward. Aliocha ducks into the washroom heart beating hard, dives under the tap to drink the non-potable water, neck bent over the edge of the basin, cheek bruised by the tap and eyes half-closed, stays there a long time with water dribbling into his ear, down his chin and onto his shirt, a long time, forgetting everything. He drinks until he's no longer thirsty. When he stands up again he takes a piss and then lights a cigarette, takes three drags, that's enough, and throws the butt into the toilet bowl. And then he opens the door a crack, looks left and right, makes sure no one is in the hall, then opens it all the way and sees, right there in front of him, the sign he had looked for in vain on the walls in the third-class car: the list of stations and timetable for the line. He goes closer, trembling, slides his finger quickly down the column beginning at Irkutsk, and murmurs, as his finger lowers: Slyudyanka, Mysovsk, Ulan-Ude,

Zaudinskiy, Onokhoi, Petrovsky-Zavod, Khilok, Mogzon, Chita, Darasun, Karymskaya. . . Chita! His finger stops. He remembers hearing this name in soldiers' boasting, towards the beginning of the journey, a little after Nijni Novgorod or maybe around Kazan, he can't remember. But he knows Chita: it was the "city of exiles"— the Decembrists were deported there in 1825 after the failed coup d'état against the Tsar—before becoming a "closed city" during the Cold War. In other words, closure and secrecy, everything that haunts and freezes him. Today it's still a military place, a garrison town— China is so close and fear of an invasion is still alive. We're getting off in Chita, Aliocha concludes, alarmed, that's what the others were talking about, that's where the barracks are. After Chita he notes a pictogram in the shape of a fork indicating that the railway divides in two, the Trans-Manchurian line breaking free from the Trans-Siberian to head south towards Beijing via Harbin. Aliocha concentrates, notes the kilometer indications and calculates the time he has left, about twelve hours from here to Chita, he has to get out of here before then, gets confused, starts the count over again, goes back up the column of names and lands on Ulan-Ude. It's a big city, the Buryat capital, two hoops of fire thrown into a leather sky, that's where he'll get out. It will be four-thirty in the morning.

ÉLÈNE HAD pushed back her sheets and sat up in her bunk when she heard him go out. She checks the compartment with a circular sweep of her eye, considering the new privacy of the room and the disorder that reigns: books on the ground, laptop open, sheets of paper, makeup tubes and clothes scattered about. She catches sight of the fatigues in a ball on the ground—she has to get rid of them—and the bag of food open on the table—he would have been hungry, of course. She doesn't turn on the overhead light but lifts the curtain of the big window where everything is black and magmatic, and where she sees nothing but herself. The large-format portrait of a woman in full flight on a train somewhere in the middle of Siberia. What's this story all about? she asks herself, very calm, causing the shadows on her face to shift in the glow of the nightlight, carving out her features in a strange cinema of black and white—serpentine flashes in the curls of her hair, milky forehead, pits of her eye sockets of a very pure black, marble cheekbones accenting hollowed cheeks, carbon lips. It's the midway point of the night and she is hyper-lucid here, she looks her situation up and down— the absurdity of it—boarding the first train that passed, all she's doing is getting further from her destination— who would be crazy enough to go from Krasnoyarsk to Vladivostok in order to get back to Paris? Why? Lifting her eyes, she sees Aliocha watching her in the reflection. He's back, shirt soaked and cheeks red. She smiles.

Then there's a knock at the door and a voice calls out "Ulan-Ude!" The same knocks and the same voice can be heard, growing quieter, down the train car. Hélène and Aliocha jump and look at each other, dumb-founded: she hadn't changed her watch, which still says three-thirty when it should be an hour later. Blindsided, petrified, they listen to the familiar tempo of the train, slowing now, and soon stopping. But it's not the usual agitation of night stops, the whispers that accompany the sound of suitcases being dragged along, voices of children stammering their dreams: heavy, sharp steps can be heard, cavalcades of big boots. Rays of light sweep through the compartment, Hélène and Aliocha dive, a shared reflex, they lift their heads just enough for their eyes to see outside where the lit-up platform gives them a nightmare vision: haggard, not yet sobered up, and clumsy, the conscripts tumble out and line up on the platform, buttoning their jackets, their gear at their feet, panicked under the shouts of a big guy in uniform pants so tight they look like leotards, and this way of walking, slow, rolling exaggeratedly over the ball of the foot, this pleasure in displaying his power—Letchov. He looks over the first row, teeth clenched but eyes drifting over the faces as though he was taking his sweet time to choose his victim, probably wanting to take revenge on the brothers, the cousins, the friends of all those little shits who flock to his sweetheart the minute he goes out to the field. He returns to the first row and kicks a bag with clothes and packs of smokes hanging out. Aliocha's backpack. Behind Hélène, the boy has stopped breathing.

The door slides open behind them, it's the brown-haired *provodnitsa* who dives headfirst into the compartment, spewing Russian at top speed, grabs Aliocha by the wrist and pulls him into the corridor, everything happens very fast, hurry, hurry up, this is what she seems to be saying to the boy who goes along without understanding a thing, doesn't want to believe it—they were supposed to get off in Chita, in Chita, not here, why Ulan-Ude?—while Hélène stays frozen in the middle of her compartment. The hostess and the boy go together along the six or seven meters of corridor and reach the door of the washrooms where she pushes him inside, tells him to close the door but not lock it, then turns around, comes back to Hélène who hasn't moved a millimeter, gives her a sign to lay back down, authoritarian, shh, go back to sleep! Less than two minutes pass before new knocks sound on the doors, insults, invectives. The conscripts have spread out and are searching the train, two per car, Hélène opens the door and, it's awful, as soon as they're inside they turn to check directly inside the cavity above the door, inspecting the hole where Aliocha had hidden before. Then they search through everything, ignoring Hélène who had just stuffed Aliocha's fatigues into the pillowcase, the fabric of which is so thin, though, that you can see the camouflage print right through it. Heart hammering in her chest she ends up sitting down on it, legs crossed nonchalantly, and displays the face of an outraged passenger. They don't find anything, scratch their heads and go out to continue the search—the woman who wanted to swim in Lake Baikal and the eight-year-old boy so curious about prehistoric fauna are in the next compartment: woken from a dream, she curses at the two soldiers who move suitcases aside and get down on their knees to check beneath the bunks. The child cries. Hélène finally steps out and, guided by the voices she hears at the end of the corridor, walks past the open compartments one by one where passengers in pajamas, astonished and furious, rub their eyes and shift from foot to foot.

The two conscripts are there, standing before the brown-haired *provodnitsa* who's mopping the floor with her back to the washrooms, barring their way. Bucket at her feet, brush-broom in her arms, she lathers the ground with large energetic movements, diluting an excessive amount of powdered detergent, creating between them and her an impassable zone, a border river that reflects the lights of the corridor, and as she scrubs she speaks to them from her shore, occupying time as much as she occupies space. She tells the two guys she's taking advantage of the stop to clean inside the washrooms, it's no luxury, she jokes, complicit, even in first class, if you knew the shit I have to clean up, you wouldn't believe it, never seen anything like it. They snicker and ask her about the private matters of rich people, hygiene and filth: the foreigner too? The *provodnitsa* lifts her head, using the back of her wrist to push back a lock of hair that had fallen over her face: who, the French woman? She puffs up her breasts, wide smile and jovial camaraderie while inside her fear is so great she's not even sure she'll be able to remain standing, oh, she's the worst of all, she doesn't even wash! She holds her broom up like a lance, vertical, the other hand resting on her hip, and she laughs, feigning ease, I tell you guys, she hasn't washed a single time! The boys crack up too, but time is ticking and now, awkward, they ask if they can nevertheless see inside the washrooms, at which point the *provodnitsa*, admirable in her authority, orders them to stay where they are but with an ample movement opens the door for them—her movement is so perfectly measured that the door slows without banging against the inside wall, revealing, for all intents and purposes, an empty, clean space. Aliocha stands flattened behind the door and digs into the wall with the back of his head. The two guys lean over flat-backed without venturing a toe onto the clean surface, one of them stretches his chin towards the inside then straightens up again, it's all good. Joking over now, the two kids step off the train and rush to stand at attention before Letchov, reporting back.

There's no one in that car, they declare, out of breath, the skin of their faces gritty beneath the very white lights. The sergeant wants to know if they inspected the luggage compartments—Hélène, back in her compartment, watches the scene through the curtain, sees Letchov sketching in space the enclave above the door—the two conscripts nod: affirmative. Under the bunks?—new sign from Letchov and same choreography of the two others. The toilets? In the same spirit, with splendid solidarity in the half-lie, they respond in chorus, nothing to see in there either, sergeant. Click of the heels, clumsy because they still haven't done their military classes—only know the rudimentary choreography—but Letchov fumes, white with rage. Find me that little shit.

Aliocha lets himself slide down the wall inside the washroom and sits crouched, solar plexus heavy as an anvil, lips drooling and black spots passing slowly before his eyes. He concentrates with all his strength on the noises outside, the far-off voices, the echo of steps on the platform, inside the train and, so close, the scrubbing of the brush broom in the corridor, just there on the other side of the door, intimate, a caress. It's long, this hunt, long and sterile. The efforts produce nothing, and when the train starts rolling again, the boy who believes he's saved stands up a little too quickly and wavers, the black spots in front of his eyes speeding up and exploding into a thousand particles—he's so dizzy he nearly falls, catches himself on the sink but slips as he does and his shoe bangs into the metal garbage can: a sound as loud as danger. Alerted, the *provodnitsa* takes a step back and whispers an order through the half-open door, keep quiet, in fifteen minutes we'll be in Zaudinskiy, the departure station for the Trans-Mongolian, that's where they're getting out, fifteen more minutes and this will be over. Aliocha is panting now, he won't make it—fifteen minutes is an eternity for someone hiding in the washroom of a train behind a door that could bust open at any second.

The passengers woken by the commotion turn out the lights and lie back down, all except for the woman and the child who show up now in front of the washrooms. They make a funny pair: the woman is white and knobbly, an apple-green t-shirt squashing her chest, baggy jogging pants hanging down below her flat butt, white muscular arms, rotten teeth, and the boy, behind her, smelling of hay, is about eight years old and beautiful. They want sugar and hot water, they want some tea. Caught off guard, the *provodnitsa* refuses at first to leave her guard post, says she'll bring it to them later, right now she has to finish cleaning, but the woman is unbending, sugar, I need some, I'm sick. The *provodnitsa* jams her broom diagonally across the door of the washroom and walks ahead of them to the samovar, picks up a tin can and lifts the cover for them to serve themselves. It's at this exact moment that the sound of footsteps reaches her from the far end of the corridor. She leans back to see and freezes: Letchov has burst in, preceded by the guy from second class who Hélène and Aliocha had passed after Krasnoyarsk. He's pointing out the foreigner's compartment. Holding the tin of sugar tightly against her belly, she goes forward to meet them.

A quarter of an hour, fifteen kilometers. Aliocha begins to count silently, concentrating on each number, visualizing and weighing it before tossing it over his shoulder and moving on to the next, immune now to the sounds of the train that clanks at regular intervals, creating another timeline, and immune to the voices of Letchov and the creep who are holding court at the moment on the other side of the door—the man swearing he saw the two of them together, testifying to Hélène's arrogance and Aliocha's stealth, and vice versa—Aliocha is a stranger to everything that is not the stillness of his body for a quarter of an hour, for fifteen kilometers. Master the pain, operate at reduced power, slow the beating of the heart, reach a coma state where nothing else sounds or moves, where there is no more breath and not a trace of tension, become a living corpse, a thing without muscles, without nerves, without intention; do not react to any stimulation, tear each kilometer from time, one by one, all fifteen of them. Soon the seconds cease to pass, they form something like drops of oil at the surface of the water, coalescence destroys time, and while the sky over Siberia lowers a notch, Aliocha holds his breath and widens wild eyes, replaying its historic choreography, the fatal closure, a blink of an eye and it's the end, a blink of an eye and the woman in the red coat is there before him, looking at him, staggeringly beautiful, a hallucination.

Letchov and his sidekick knock on the door of the compartment and Hélène opens it, exasperated, while the *provodnitsa* catches her eye from the doorway and lowers her lids, a sign to remain calm. The two men enter, inspect, and when they find nothing, the creep swallows his anger, embarrassed—but convinced, still, that he saw a conscript follow the woman into this compartment, on my son's life. Letchov cuts him off and orders him to leave. Then it's just him and Hélène, who has turned her pillow over and hastily pulled Aliocha's t-shirt on under her pajama shirt, not knowing where to put it and not managing to open the window to toss it outside. Letchov sniffs, comes closer to her, something's off in here, he murmurs to the hostess who, to show her good will, sniffs as well, stepping towards the window as though looking for someone, abruptly seizes the bag of food from under the table, opens it with one hand while the other hand pinches her nose, look at this, it's going rotten, you mustn't keep this! She brandishes a warm packet below the sergeant's nose, full of stagnating dried fish, and he turns away in disgust. He plants himself in front of Hélène and takes his time looking her over—time which once again drips and becomes suspended, the space under pressure that swells and balloons—he stretches a white hand with feminine nails towards the duvet, pulls the fabric toward him, a sharp movement that reveals the folds of the sheet, their suspicious rumpled state, raises his eyes to Hélène who doesn't blink—but under her shirt is Aliocha's shirt like a second skin, with its numbered label that rubs against her neck and she crosses her arms over her chest to slow the rush of her heart. She stays like this, completely still even though she's on the verge of exploding, until Letchov finally smiles, clicks his heels, and steps back out into the corridor, spitting on the ground.

And then everything speeds up, an acceleration that no one could have predicted. Because instead of continuing their round, Letchov and the creep retrace their steps and pause right outside the washrooms, take out cigarettes and lighters, and right at that moment, hurtling along like an elf, the eight-year-old boy weaves between them and without asking anyone anything he pushes open the door to the washroom and goes in. The horrified *provodnitsa* lets out a scream and drops the sugar tin which bounces on the ground in a metallic crash and in the same moment the child's eyes grow wider than dinner plates as Aliocha's hand covers his mouth—the conscript had leapt to his feet the second the kid came in, locking the door with one hand while muzzling the boy with the other and then pinning him against the sink. Now he speaks quietly into his neck, threats of death in a barely-audible breath, if you shout I'll break your head, I'll kill you, I'll strangle you, and the child begins to cry, tears of terror that stream down his cheeks and drip onto Aliocha's hand whose face is so close to the child's that their noses brush against each other. After a few seconds, when the child has stopped struggling, Aliocha loosens his grip and whispers, you'll take a piss and you'll wash your hands, you'll leave and go back to bed without saying anything to anyone, not even to your mother or else I'll kill you both—and again, he presses tight against the child's mouth before finally taking his hand away.

The boy turns to the toilet and starts to pee—he swallows his tears silently, shoulders shaking, frail and pointed, very white, locks of hair standing up in cowlicks on top of his head. Behind him Aliocha fights to keep his fury intact, not to let himself be moved, to remain ready to strike. It's long, a neverending tinkle, and Aliocha gets impatient, hurry up. Three knocks on the door show him he's right, the voice of the *provodnitsa*, everything OK, little one? Behind her, Letchov and the creep can be heard talking about the deserter. Aliocha whispers to the child to answer, *da, da,* the little trembling voice—he flushes the toilet and washes his hands. Your face too, splash some water on your face, Aliocha commands, thinking the tears will mix with it. Then while the water is still running, Aliocha unlocks the door and the child slips out, the *provodnitsa* doesn't come in but sticks a hand inside to turn off the tap and takes the child by the wrist to bring him back to his compartment, passing Letchov, still smoking, and the creep who teases the kid, scrawny little Rubin Kazan fan—those guys are no winners, kid, the masters are in Spartak.

The train stops. Zaudinskiy. A backwater platform on the outskirts of Ulan-Ude and the fork towards the Mongolian steppe. Again, the roll call, the kit they have to drag with them, the straight rows and search reports, the speech for the occasion and the empty hours to wait before boarding the Trans-Mongolian for Naushki on the Chinese border, and again there's Letchov planted in the center, feet in dancer's position and hands behind his back, spitting out a speech with exaggerated coldness and insult, a conscript has deserted, all leaves are cancelled, you're all worthless little shits, but the conscripts don't care, don't protest—barely a tensing of jaws or throbbing of veins in the temples—leaves are not for them, they don't even have the means to go home, they're saving their money for the last trip, the return trip, when all this will be over and they'll be able to board the Trans-Siberian in the opposite direction. After ten minutes, the train sets off, scrolls past the recruits who have broken rank and stand scattered on the platform, and as it leaves the station, silence falls over the length of it.

AND THEN Hélène goes out into the corridor to find the *provodnitsa* and together they go to open the door for Aliocha. They don't see him right away, he's not standing behind the door anymore, he's huddled on the ground like a thing the tremors of terror have emptied of substance, a hidden thing, that has brutalized a woman, terrorized a child, a thing that was ready to kill so it wouldn't be caught—he thinks back to the exact impulse of his palm against the boy's lips and sees again the artery pulsating along the small white neck.

Hélène goes in first, come, it's over, you can come out, placing a hand on his unmoving shoulder. Aliocha doesn't get up, keeps his head against his knees, body shriveled up, pressed against the toilet bowl, nose near the odors of urine, it's over, it's ok, she murmurs. After a long moment, the young man slowly lifts his face towards the two women, a face bathed in tears. The *provodnitsa* steps back slowly and Hélène crouches down beside him, puts an arm around his shoulders, and now their heads are touching; they remain like this for a long time, side by side, head to head, a long time, as the day breaks, for it's dawn now, as the train chugs along, this engine of iron that materializes time; they keep their eyes lowered, they haven't yet seen the velvet expanse of the landscape, the grassy ground, a prairie shaken by winds, and they remain conjoined for long minutes. When they do get up, slowly, and appear in the mirror, they are deathly pale, dirty hair and dry lips, they look like hell. Outlaws, you'd say, survivors. Hélène faces him and begins a strange ballet. In finely tuned movements, she unbuttons his shirt, then turns him very gently to face the sink, lean over, she murmurs, and he places his forearms on either side of the basin. She turns on the tap and picks up an abandoned cup, pours ice cold water over his shoulders and the back of his neck—he doesn't start or shiver, he keeps his eyes closed, lean over more, the young man leans further over, water streaming over his head, down his temples and dripping along his brow ridges. She takes a sliver of soap so thin it's transparent and washes his shoulders, his back, a creamy, pale foam she rinses off with more water, and soon they're floundering. And then he straightens up, blood flowing back into his face—he's another person, and it's Hélène's turn now. Wordlessly she takes off her shirt and the khaki t-shirt Aliocha recognizes, leans over the sink with her arms crossed over her breasts, and Aliocha officiates with sure hands, supple and cold fingers that find their bearings beneath her hairline. The *provodnitsa* has side-stepped this baptism to go back to her compartment and resume her post. Finally, silently, they get dressed again, and with water still streaming from their faces and their clothes they return to the compartment to lie down, each on a bunk, hands joined and arms forming a bridge above the void until they let go and fall asleep.

The silence is what wakes them, silence and stillness. They don't know what day it is or what time. A cerulean sky burnishes the Trans-Siberian, stopped in open countryside, and Hélène looks out the window at the travelers who have stepped off to smoke a cigarette or simply breathe the evening air on Buryat lands—among them, many are now men and women with round faces, vinyl-black hair and pale ochre skin. She recognizes the Baikal fanatics, the child and the woman from the next compartment. Aliocha stands up and smiles, shall we go outside?—he signs his question with precision, his eyes and hands flutter—shall we take a little walk? Hélène nods, and out they go.

Touching the earth for the first time since Krasnoyarsk,

Hélène wobbles, nauseous and exhilarated. The desire to run. She's already moving away from the tracks, doesn't see Aliocha and the child lock eyes behind her, Aliocha daring a gentle look and placing a finger over his lips as the terrified child slips behind his mother; she also doesn't see that the creep from second class has just watched them get out, stupefied, not recognizing the conscript anymore in the young man in a white shirt, and trying to get a better look at his face. Hélène finally turns around, calls out, Aliocha, come, come, and they run, in small steps at first as they start to climb the hill, leaving the train behind them, the crowded corridors and the hunt, taking large strides now; the air is cold, dry, the grass hard, but they climb as though they were headed to a party, in a hurry to see what the other side will reveal, and little by little they rise. It seems to them that space rushes into them, airs them out and smothers them, propelling them forward. By the time they reach the top, it's almost nightfall, the electricity of the sky has changed to a muted gleaming and the hillside that rushes down below their feet is exactly the same emerald green as the virgin forest, a suffocation of living matter, and they melt into it, together. The silence is so great after the din of the train that each sound explodes, lives its life of noise, a screech of grasses, a rustle of feathers, a slab of earth cracking, the echo of their presence beneath the sky that fills now with ink, all soundings that are like the dorsal fin of space, and their voices too are of another material. Because they're talking now, stirring their tongues like shamans, Aliocha turning in a circle and pointing out the four cardinal directions, reciting: to the north, the Yakut people and the diamonds hidden deep under the ground, the Nenets people and reindeer meat devoured raw on the tundra; pointing out the Russian Far East—extended arm of the weather vane—and Ussuri, at the edge of the Sea of Japan, the tropical rainforest and the animal world in the brightness of its reign, wild cats and martens, to the south, cavalcades of horses, caravans, encampments, and to the west, what? To the west is France! They roar with laughter. Hélène catches only the flow of new energy but has started to sing, her voice is sure, drawing loops in the evening air, Anton's song, and Aliocha recognizes it, takes it up with her, happy, the east wind rises and sweeps the hat off the rebel peasant, and truly, to see them from the train at the base of the hill, you'd think they were burning up with joy—like torches, the great drunkenness that comes after the danger.

The ocean appears on the dawn of the last day. Forty kilometers to Vladivostok—it's the end of the journey. Hélène is sure of nothing, but far off there's this span of clarity, this sparkling, ethereal horizon, and the landscape dilates, slows, hidden in a light mist. She squints: bursts of light here and there from liquid surfaces, points of radiance that touch and meld and then it's the sea, there, to the south of the tracks, the Pacific Ocean—

which has not a trace of indigo at this latitude, nothing of Polynesian cyan, nothing turquoise or even blue: it's zinc. She lowers a hand onto Aliocha's shoulder and says softly, Aliocha, the Pacific, wake up. He opens his eyes and leaps up at once. He has never seen the sea, was expecting something more, something more spectacular, but he widens his eyes.

And then the coastline disappears, they remain silent but stay turned towards the outside, sides pressed together. Maybe they are too exhausted now to speak, the precision of gestures involving their whole bodies like a kind of gymnastics, or maybe they are beyond exhaustion, because there has been no day or night in this train since Zaudinskiy and the departure of the troops, because the times of waking and sleeping alternate in brief, irregular intervals, overlapping and mixing together, as though Hélène and Aliocha had little by little renounced the alignment of their biological clocks with the terrestrial cycle of night / day, night /

day, tick-tock-tick-tock, and something else in them had given way, freeing an unknown temporality, elastic and floating.

Their REM sleep time has been whittled down as well, so they have trouble committing to memory the things they are experiencing, remembering the station in Chita—which is a good thing: if Aliocha had retained the image of the soldiers on the platform, dazed and lost, childhood hidden in the depths of the circles under their eyes, he would simply collapse, the whole length of him, fall to the ground—or recalling the expanse that tears apart when the Siberian plains open to the north a little before Mogosha, gathering up the color of the Amur two days later in Khabarovsk, huge metal bridge the hue of rusted Coca-Cola, traffic on the river—when they see cargo ships, though, it prepares them for the approaching sea—the banks constellated with oil spills and the taiga evaporated. They don't try to cement their encounter, to sediment all that has passed between them: they trust the train, even as the rails suddenly veer south, slicing between the Chinese border and the stirring underbrush of the Ussuri, and the relief line of the landscape is like the electrocardiogram of an impatient child. The station platforms get mixed up until they form no more than a single sensory cell, the cigarette smoked in the early morning, a scalding glass of tea in hand, their disjointed journeys slowly drawing figure-eights on terra firma—and this, they store up, who could say why.

The ocean reappears later, north of Vladivostok, ashy beaches, waiting hotels, trails of hydrophilic foam on the crest of the waves and their slow, slow unrolling: the last stop is near. And then things begin to stir and rise, a confusion of concrete hills, Soviet-style apartment buildings leaning over the ocean, rarer old buildings, and finally the station. Hélène gathers up her things, Aliocha lingers, they avoid making eye contact; they leave the compartment without a glance back, get off the Trans-Siberian, it's humid and warm, they're surprised, they face each other, reeling, at a loss for what to do, what to say or give to each other—as though only the train's movement could activate their language, as though outside of the train, outside of the escape, there were no more movements to make, no more songs—as though everything had to finally come to a stop. Come, let's take a photo. With a tightness in her throat Hélène holds onto Aliocha who puffs up his chest—they hold each other side by side, posing together, it's the *provodnitsa* who photographs them before embracing them together, and on the screen, they look like each other, they have the same faces.

archipelago books
is a not-for-profit literary press devoted to
promoting cross-cultural exchange through innovative
classic and contemporary international literature
www.archipelagobooks.org